The Red Dragons of Gressingham

by

Philip Ardagh

Illustrated by Mike Phillips

You do not need to read this page – just get on with the book!

First published in 2008 in Great Britain by
Barrington Stoke Ltd
18 Walker St, Edinburgh, EH3 7LP

www.barringtonstoke.co.uk

ISBN: 978-1-84299-538-9

Printed in Great Britain by Bell & Bain Ltd

AUTHOR ID

Name: Philip Ardagh

Likes: Smiling, good books and Cornish ice cream.

Dislikes: Salt and vinegar crisps, cold showers and rude people.

3 words that best describe me:
Big, fat, bearded.

A secret that not many people know:
I'm not very good at spelling.

ILLUSTRATOR ID

Name: Mike Phillips

Likes: Cricket, books and my comfy chair.

Dislikes: Exercise, vegetables and sand in my shorts.

3 words that best describe me:
Short, round, fun.

A secret that not many people know:
Don't tell anyone, but under my hat I've got no hair!!

For Butterscotch, Rex, Mumble and Softy

Contents

Introduction

Meet the Green Men of Gressingham. The Green Men were a band of robbers and outlaws when Gressingham was ruled by the evil Marshal Guppy. Now that Lord Dashwood is back in charge at the castle, they have no one to fight and nothing to do ... until his lordship comes up with a plan. He will send them on a special quest. But is all quite as it seems?

Chapter 1
The Big Yawn

Big Jim was bored. Fidget was bored. Friendly was bored. In fact, *all* of the Green Men of Gressingham were bored. They hung around the forest yawning.

Fidget was fidgeting. Friendly was trying to make friends with an ant, and Big Jim was leaning against a tree. Big Jim was big, but the tree was even bigger. Much bigger. This was their look-out tree. They used the tree to look out for their enemies, in the days when they were outlaws. Now they didn't have any enemies to look out for. They hung their washing on the tree instead.

The roundest of all the Green Men was Physic. He was busy hanging clothes on the branches to dry. They were all brown. This was because the Green Men all wore brown. Brown hid the dirt better than green, and they didn't wash their clothes *that* often.

"I'm so bored," said Physic hanging the last brown sock on the tree.

"Me too," said Big Jim. "I wish some robbers would come into the forest and we could have a good old punch-up."

"We haven't had a fight for a long, long time," said Fidget.

"A long, long, long, *long* time," added Friendly (who was the one Green Man who didn't like fighting much anyway).

"Why don't we have a bow-and-arrow contest?" suggested Lanky. He was almost as tall as Big Jim but was very, very, *very* thin.

"We did that yesterday." Friendly yawned.

"How about a pie-eating contest?" said Physic.

The other Green Men stared at Physic's great big tummy. "We did that the day *before* yesterday," said Big Jim.

"And you always win!" said Fidget.

Physic grinned. "I do, don't I?" he said. Physic loved pies.

"We could tidy the camp?" Friendly suggested. He had given up on the ant and was now being friendly to a buttercup.

"We are outlaws!" shouted Big Jim. "Outlaws don't do housework!"

"We're not outlaws any more," Friendly reminded him. "Now we are *in*-laws. We are on the same side as the law now that Marshal Guppy has been locked up."

Big Jim frowned. "That's true," he said at last. "But I still don't like housework!"

"Hard luck," said Physic, "because it's your turn to feed Martha."

Martha was the Green Men's pet pig. She was very big and very pink. It was hard to tell that she was pink because she loved to roll in the mud. She always looked as brown as the Green Men's clothes.

Big Jim muttered something under his breath. He picked up a bucket of acorns and went over to the pig pen. He didn't mind really. He was very fond of Martha and feeding her gave him something to do.

The pig pen was empty.

"Martha has gone!" he shouted.

"Gone?" shouted the others.

"Gone!" said Big Jim.

The others rushed over to see what he was talking about. Big Jim was right. The muddy pig was nowhere to be seen.

Chapter 2
Under Attack

"How did Martha get out?" Friendly wondered. "The gate to the pig pen is still closed."

"She's been stolen!" said Physic. He looked very upset. He loved Martha. He even ate like her.

"You were hoping for robbers in the forest, Big Jim!" said Lanky.

"And now we've got at least one," said Fidget. "A pig thief!"

The smallest of all the Green Men was called Squat. He picked up a sword and waved it above his head. This wasn't hard because most things were above his head anyway. And it was a very large sword. "We must find the thief and get Martha back!" he shouted.

At that moment, something stung Squat's neck. He dropped the sword in surprise. It stuck in the ground like King Arthur's sword in the stone. "Ouch!" he said.

"What's wrong?" asked Big Jim. Then something stung him on the cheek. "Ouch!!!" he shouted.

"What –?" began Friendly. Now something stung *him* on the head.

"Shhh!" said Fidget. He pointed to a clump of bushes.

The Green Men stopped to listen. Big Jim pulled the sword out of the ground. Lanky picked up his bow and pulled out an arrow from the quiver on his back. Physic grabbed his staff (which was a very long stick). Squat picked up a stone.

There were sounds coming from the bushes. They sounded like someone trying very hard not to laugh.

"Come on out!" shouted Big Jim. "We've got you surrounded."

A head popped out above the top of the leaves. It was Tom, Lord Dashwood's nephew! Tom had helped the Green Men free Lord Dashwood from the evil clutches of Marshal Guppy, and bring peace back to Gressingham.

Tom was grinning from ear to ear. "Hello, everyone!" he said. He came out of his hiding place. In one hand he was holding a piece of rope. In the other he was holding a peashooter. The Green Men put down their weapons.

"So that's what the stinging was!" Big Jim laughed. "You were shooting dried peas at us!"

"What a waste," Physic said with a sigh. "They would make a nice soup."

Now Tom laughed. "Trust you to be thinking of your tummy!" he said. He tugged the rope and Martha came out from behind the bush. "Call yourself a bunch of outlaws? I stole Martha from right under your noses."

"We're not really outlaws anymore," Friendly reminded him with a grin.

"And Martha would have squealed if she didn't know you!" said Big Jim.

The Green Men were pleased to see Tom. Now that he was a page boy, they didn't see him very often. They all sat around the camp fire and asked him for any news. Physic put on a pot of water to boil to make some nettle tea.

"How are things at Dashwood Castle?" asked Friendly.

"How is your training going?" asked Fidget. "Will you be a knight soon?"

"No." Tom put his head in his hands and sighed. "I'm beginning to think I'll be a page boy forever." Then his face brightened. He smiled. "But I have good news for you! My uncle, Lord Dashwood, has summoned you all to Dashwood Castle!"

Chapter 3
To the Castle Once More

The men set off for the castle at once.
That night they slept at *The Swan Inn*, under
the sign of the blue bull. (Don't ask.) The
following morning, the in-laws set off again.
They were met by a woman on a beautiful
jet-black horse.

"Robyn!" called out a delighted Tom. It
was Robyn-in-the-Hat, leader of the Green
Men. Tom rode up along side her. "It's good to
see you again," he said.

"You too, Master Tom," she replied. She was called Robyn-in-the-Hat because of the strange hat she wore. It was half hat and half mask. A felt flap came down over the top part of her face. There were two holes through which you could see her sparkling blue eyes.

Robyn used to wear the hat to hide her true identity. Now that the Green Men were no longer outlaws, many people thought she would stop wearing it, but she didn't. "The secret must remain," she had said.

"Do you know what your uncle, Lord Dashwood, wants with you all?" she asked. "Is Gressingham in danger again?"

"No danger," said Tom. "He said he has a surprise for you."

"And you don't know what it is?"

Tom shook his head. "It will be a surprise for me too."

"I don't like surprises," said Fidget, who was trotting on his horse behind them.

They reached Dashwood Castle many hours later. The soldier on look-out duty on the battlements of the castle gatehouse saw the Green Men long before they reached the gate. By the time they arrived, a small crowd was there to greet them. Tom's friend Able Morris stood in the front wearing his favourite hat.

"Greetings, Tom!" he said. "I see you found our fearless friends."

"Yes," said Tom as he jumped down from his horse. "And they are as eager as I am to find out what my uncle wants them for."

"They will find out soon enough," said Able. "You are all to go to the great hall at once."

Just as soon as their horses had been led
to the castle stables, Tom led Robyn-in-the-
Hat and the Green Men to the great hall.
Tom's uncle, Lord Dashwood, was sitting in a
big wooden chair at the far end. He stood up
when they came in.

"Welcome," he said. "I've been waiting for
you!"

Chapter 4
The Plan Unfolds

"I want you to go to the Red Rock Mountains," boomed Lord Dashwood. "You too, Tom."

Tom was amazed. "But no one goes to the Red Rock Mountains, uncle!" he said.

"Not if they can help it," muttered Fidget.

"We'll need to take plenty of supplies, your lordship!" said Physic, already planning some menus in his head.

"It could be – er – dangerous, sire," Friendly added.

"I thought you *liked* danger," said Lord Dashwood.

"Like it? We live for it, my lord," said Robyn-in-the-Hat. Tom could see her eyes sparkling with excitement.

"There's just the small matter of the dragons," said Squat.

"Who said that?" asked Lord Dashwood. He leant forward in his throne-like chair.

Squat stepped out of Big Jim's big shadow. "Me, your Lordship."

"And you think dragons are just a *small* matter?" asked Lord Dashwood. He looked around the great hall at all the other Green Men. "If the smallest man among you thinks dragons are just a small matter, then I know I've chosen the right people!"

Squat wanted to point out that he was only joking. He thought dragons would be a very big problem indeed!

"Chosen us for what?" asked Tom.

"For a quest, of course. I want you to go to the Red Rock Mountains *and bring me back a dragon*."

Now it wasn't just Tom who was amazed. Everyone was, apart from Lord Dashwood, of course. He was busy grinning behind his great big moustache.

"A dragon quest!" said Robyn-in-the-Hat. "It will be an honour, my lord!"

"But what do you need a dragon for?" asked Friendly.

"Forgive the men, my lord," said Robyn. Tom guessed that she was frowning *hard* at Friendly from behind her mask. "We relish the challenge of bringing you back a dragon."

"You did say *dragon*, didn't you, my lord?" asked Fidget. "One of those giant, lizard-like, fire-breathing monsters?"

"The very same," said Lord Dashwood with a nod.

"But don't they eat people?" asked Friendly. "I'm sure I heard somewhere that they eat people."

"Baron Hankey tells me that he has one over in Woolton," said Lord Dashwood. "He didn't say anything about it eating anybody."

"When do we start, your lordship?" asked Big Jim. Anything was better than sitting around twiddling his thumbs.

"After a large meal?" Physic suggested.

The great hall echoed with Lord Dashwood's booming laughter. "What an excellent idea!" he said.

Chapter 5
Meet the Expert

After a very fine meal, they made plans. There were no maps of the Red Rock Mountains themselves. This was because so few people had been there. Or because those who had gone there had never come back. However, there were maps showing the best ways to *reach* the mountains. The tables had been cleared and the maps laid on them.

"What's that squiggle?" Friendly pointed.

"I think it's a stream," said Able Morris. He took a closer look at the map.

"And that big round thing?" asked Friendly.

"I think that's supposed to be a big round rock," said Able Morris.

"And that thing which looks like a squashed fly?"

Tom leant in very close. He scratched the latest mark on the map that Friendly was pointing at. "It *is* a squashed fly," he said.

"This map reading business is real easy!" Friendly laughed.

"That may be so," said Lord Dashwood, "but I have asked a dragon expert to join you on your quest. His name is Dredwich." He turned to Able Morris and spoke in his ear.

Able nodded his head and hurried out of the great hall. His squashy hat bobbed on the top of his head as he walked. He returned moments later with a man dressed in a dark, hooded robe. The man smelled strongly of earthy toadstools and soggy mushrooms.

He bowed before the Lord of Dashwood Castle, who introduced him to the others. "This is Dredwich," he said.

"An honour to meet the Green Men of Gressingham," said Dredwich. "It is thanks to you that the evil Marshal Guppy is now locked up where he belongs. I am your humble servant and guide for this dangerous quest."

Big Jim slapped the man on the back. "If you know *anything* about dragons then you know more about dragons than the rest of us put together!" he boomed.

"Except for the eating humans part," said Friendly.

"And the big lizard-like, fire-eating part," said Squat.

"It would seem you know more about dragons than you thought," said Dredwich. He gave a wheezy cough.

"Are you a professional dragon expert?" Tom asked him. He didn't mind the smell of old toadstools.

"I am master of the unexplained and unexplainable," Dredwich wheezed.

"What do you mean by that, sire?" asked Tom.

"I can't explain," said Dredwich. "Now, I must get ready for the dragon quest." He bowed his head to Lord Dashwood again. "Good day to you all," he said. He left the

room. There was a trail of a light dusting of soil where he had walked in and out.

"An odd fellow," said Big Jim.

"He smelled of old mushrooms," said Friendly.

"I like mushrooms," said Physic, which came as no surprise to anybody.

"Me too," said Tom.

Chapter 6
All Set to Go

Tom found it hard to sleep that night. A dragon quest! What could be more exciting? His tummy felt very funny indeed. It was churning with a mixture of excitement and fear.

Most of the others felt the same at breakfast. Very few ate more than a few mouthfuls, apart from Big Jim. The reason why Physic didn't eat anything was because he wasn't there. He had been up long before the others and gone down to the castle kitchens. He had made friends with the castle's new cook. By the time breakfast came around, he had got together plenty of supplies for the quest. There were lots of sacks and barrels. All Physic had to do now was to find a way of carrying it all.

He tracked down Tom after breakfast. "Will Lord Dashwood lend us extra horses to carry our supplies?"

"I'm sure he will," Tom nodded. "After all, this is his special quest we're going on, remember? I'll speak to Able about it."

Tom spoke to Able and Able spoke to Mr Nuzzle who was in charge of the castle's stables. This was a very important job. One of the things that set apart knights from foot soldiers was that knights rode horses. A knight couldn't be a proper knight without a horse, so horses needed looking after. That's what Mr Nuzzle did. He even looked like a horse.

Able Morris told Mr Nuzzle about the Green Men's need for more horses.

"There is one slight problem, sire," said Mr Nuzzle. "Sir Flayling's horse is lame, and we only have two spare."

"Very well," said Able Morris.

"But I could also offer them Stubborn."

"Stubborn?" asked Able.

"Stubborn," nodded Mr Nuzzle.

"Isn't Stubborn a mule?" he asked.

Mr Nuzzle nodded again.

"A very *stubborn* mule?" asked Able.

"Yes, sire," said Mr Nuzzle. "Hence the name."

"Hence the name," Able muttered.

A mule has a donkey for a father and a horse for a mother. There is a saying 'as stubborn as a mule'. Can you guess why that is? Yup. You're right. Mules can be very stubborn. They only do something if they want to do it.

Giving a mule the name Stubborn must mean that it was a very stubborn mule indeed.

"She'll have to do," Able sighed. "Please get her and the two horses ready."

"Right away, sire," said Mr Nuzzle. He called for the nearest stable boy, who came scurrying out of the straw.

Chapter 7
Away at Last

Lord Dashwood was in his private room. He had a visitor.

"You are clear on your duties?" he asked the hooded figure of Dredwich.

"Yes, your lordship. To keep Robyn-in-the-Hat and the others away from the castle as long as possible."

"Exactly!" said Lord Dashwood. "I don't care what lies you tell them or false trails you lead them on, but you must keep them away from here at all costs. Is that understood?"

"Perfectly, your lordship. Perfectly."

"Splendid. Good luck."

"Thank you, your lordship." Dredwich opened the door and walked out into the corridor, leaving his tell-tale trail of soil behind him.

****

Many members of the castle household came out to cheer off Robyn-in-the Hat, the Green Men (in brown), Tom and their expert guide. It wasn't every day that people set off on a quest to the Red Rock Mountains, let alone to bring back a dragon.

Suddenly three trumpets were sounded and Lord Dashwood appeared on the battlements of the gatehouse. The crowds cheered. He put up his hands and made a short speech about the dangers ahead. When he had finished, the crowd cheered again. The portcullis was raised and the drawbridge was lowered across the moat. Robyn-in-the-Hat led the way on her fine black horse. Soon all that could be heard was the clatter of hooves on the bridge.

Stubborn the mule refused to move. Everyone stopped.

They tried pushing.

They tried pulling.

They even tried carrots.

In the end she did follow the others but only if Friendly walked along side her, whispering into her ear.

Lord Dashwood made his way down the stone spiral staircase. Able Morris was close behind.

"Now they're out of the way we can get down to the really important matters!" he said.

Chapter 8
Strange Happenings

The first week of the dragon quest was a bit of a let down. Everyone was keen to get to the mountains but it was simply a matter of covering the ground. They passed through farms and towns and villages and were made welcome wherever they went. Because they were going about the country on official business, they were carrying a standard bearing the Dashwood coat of arms. A standard is a kind of flag. The Dashwood coat of arms was a special design made for the

Dashwood family. Dashwood's knights had it painted on their shields and wore it over their breast-plates or chain-mail. That way, everyone knew that they were loyal to Lord Dashwood. Carrying his standard meant that the Green Men went under his protection.

Not that the Green Men needed protection. These were peaceful times. All of the lords were on friendly terms at the time of the dragon quest. There was no in-fighting or sneaky goings-on. When they passed one village, a group of children threw vegetables at them but Physic was delighted. He jumped down off his horse and picked them up in his arms.

"These will make a hearty soup!" he declared.

At that moment a farmer appeared and grabbed one of the children, yanking him away by the ear. The others ran off, laughing, as fast as their legs could carry them.

Apart from that, the only other piece of real excitement was on the fourth day. That was when some locals were foolish enough to try to rob them. Before they knew what was happening, Big Jim had knocked two of them over with his staff. Physic was sitting on a third, and four others were being tied up by the other Green Men. All of them were left in a pile on the road-side wishing that they had chosen any career other than robbery.

43

When the week was over, though, things got interesting. It was time to use the maps and get off the beaten track. Now the Green Men wouldn't be following paths at all.

The mountains had seemed a long way away for much of their journey. They were still far off but were beginning to look that much closer. Now Tom believed that they really were getting nearer. He could see the redness of the rocks that gave the mountains their name.

That night they all made camp in what the map called *Ye Woods* but which was more like a big clump of trees. (Tom could read quite a few words and write his own name.)

Physic prepared a meal over the campfire and the others stared into the flames. As usual, the talk turned to dragons.

"Grubs up!" said Physic, giving the big cooking pot a final stir over the flames.

"Excellent!" said Big Jim. "What is it? I'm starving!"

"I just told you," said Physic. "It's grubs. Grub stew!"

Suddenly, Tom didn't feel so hungry. Grubs was just another word for creepy-crawlies. He would rather go to bed hungry.

Chapter 9
The Red Rocks

The next day the Green Men reached the foot-hills of the mountains. There was much excitement and cheering and Physic handed everyone an extra bun. He had made them a while back so they were quite stale. Very stale, in fact. In fact, they were almost as hard as some of the small red rocks scattered about them.

"I nearly broke a tooth!" Big Jim complained. He threw his bun at Physic. Luckily it missed him. It could have done the ex-outlaw some serious damage!

"They are not that bad," said Friendly. The truth be told, he couldn't get his teeth into his bun either.

"Forget the buns!" shouted Squat. "What's that?" He pointed up the mountain.

Tom looked halfway up the mountain. He tried to work out exactly where the smallest of the Green Men was pointing. He couldn't see anything at first. Just plenty of rocks and a few trees. Then he saw it: a puff of smoke.

"There must be someone up there ahead of us," said Tom.

"Or some*thing*," groaned Fidget. He started to fidget. "That could be dragon smoke."

Big Jim called over Dredwich.

"Could that be dragon's breath?" Big Jim asked, pointing at the smoke.

"It could be," said the so-called dragon expert. At first, he sounded unsure. Then he sounded most enthusiastic. "Most probably. In truth, most definitely. Indeed! A very fine example. Typical, in fact."

"So we can take that as a yes?" said Tom.

"Yes," said Dredwich from inside the hood of his cloak. "We're on the right track!"

"Come on, then!" said Big Jim, getting together his belongings. "Let's catch ourselves one dragon!"

Chapter 10
Where Be Dragons?

Now, *you* know that there are dragons in this story and *I* know that there are dragons in this story. There is the word 'dragons' in the title and there's even a picture of dragons on the cover. But the Green Men of Gressingham could not find any. They searched for days. And nights. They climbed high into the mountains and deep into the valleys. They searched caves and looked behind big round rocks. Dredwich kept on finding 'clues' that none of the others seemed to see or understand. He led them here, there and everywhere for days on end.

And what did they find? Nothing. Not a sausage. (And Physic would have been pleased with a sausage or two. They were running out of supplies.)

In the end, Robyn called them all together. "We have done our best," she said. "No one can do more. It is time to return to Lord Dashwood empty handed."

Tom was feeling down. He had failed his first quest!

"Not to worry," said Dredwich, who seemed quite cheerful. "If there were any dragons here we would have found them. I am sure Lord Dashwood will understand that. It will be good to get back to Dashwood Castle."

"I can't say that I mind not having come face to face with a fire-breathing man-eating monster," Squat confessed.

"Call yourself an outlaw?" Big Jim boomed.

"An *in*-law," Lanky reminded him. "We act within the law now."

Everyone put a brave face on it, but the Green Men began their long trek home with heavy hearts.

Physic and Friendly collected a few of the strange small round rocks which littered the mountain side. Each was about the size and shape of a football (when someone finally got around to inventing the game hundreds of years later).

"What do you want those for?" asked Tom.

"They'll make good souvenirs," said Friendly.

"And are proof that we actually went to the Red Rock Mountains," Fidget added. The rocks were a very strange red colour indeed.

"And few people can claim to have been to these mountains and come back safely!" agreed Big Jim. The thought seemed to cheer him up a little.

"And I've made a map of everywhere we went," said Tom. "That's never been done before either!"

"So we've much to be proud of, even if we don't return with a dragon," said Robyn. She tried to sound as positive as possible.

Even less happened on the journey back to Dashwood Castle than on their journey to the Red Rock Mountains. Most of the villages they passed were oddly empty. When, days later, Dashwood Castle came into view, there was no one to welcome them.

"I'm glad about that," said Fidget, fidgeting in his saddle. "The fewer people who see us come back without a dragon, the better."

"I shall ride ahead and tell Lord Dashwood that you failed," said Dredwich.

"That *we* failed," said Big Jim. "You failed too, Dredwich."

"And you're the expert," muttered Physic.

"Er, yes. Quite," said Dredwich. He dug his heels into the flanks of his horse and galloped off to the castle.

Chapter 11
A Wild Goose Chase?

When the rest of the party arrived back at the castle, they were in for a surprise. As they went through the gatehouse into the castle court-yard they couldn't believe their eyes. There were flags and banners and pennants everywhere. The hooves of their horses were silenced by a thick carpet, laid over the cobble-stones. Lord Dashwood himself was hurrying down the outer steps from his private rooms.

"Welcome! Welcome!" He beamed. He stretched his arms open wide.

Robyn-in-the-Hat jumped off her fine black horse and bowed. "Dredwich has told you that we failed, my lord?" she asked.

Lord Dashwood smiled. "You did not fail me," he said. "It is more that Dredwich succeeded."

"I don't understand, uncle," said Tom.

"The quest for a dragon was a wild goose chase ... Nothing more than a trick to get you away from the castle."

"You didn't really want a dragon?" asked Tom.

"I would love a dragon, but I'm not even sure that they exist!" said his uncle.

"But what about your dragon expert, sire?" asked Robyn.

"Dredwich? He is no dragon expert. He is my friend Lord Hankey's gardener! I had him play the part."

"Nothing but a gardener," muttered Tom. That explained the smell of mushrooms and the trail of soil! "But why did you want us out of the way, uncle?" he asked.

"So that we could get ready."

"Get ready? Get ready for what, your lordship?" asked Big Jim.

"For your reward for saving me from the clutches of the evil Marshal Guppy," said Lord Dashwood.

"Are you going to throw another feast?" asked Physic. He had fond memories of the last one.

"There will be much feasting, Physic. You can be sure of that. But I want to reward you all in a more lasting way, now that I am fully well again."

"How, uncle?" asked Tom.

"You are to be made a squire, Tom. You will no longer be a humble page boy. You have worked hard and earned the title."

Tom glowed with pride.

"The rest of you –" Lord Dashwood paused and looked at Big Jim, Physic, Fidget, Squat, Lanky and the others. "You are to become my knights."

They all gasped as one.

"Lords, ladies, townsfolk and villagers have been travelling far and wide to be here for your special day, which will be tomorrow."

There was a cry from Friendly, who ran into the court-yard. He had been walking next to Stubborn the mule, who had been weighed down by the round red rocks. They had only just entered the castle, a long way behind the others.

"One's hatching!" Friendly cried.

"Hatching?" asked Tom.

"Hatching!" cried Friendly. He was holding up one of the football-shaped red rocks. It did, indeed, appear to be hatching.

A moment later, the top of the rock broke off and out poked the head of a tiny dragon.

Yes. *Out poked the head of a tiny dragon.*

The little dragon flapped its stubby wings and flew up into the air. It made a sneezing sound and flames shot out of its nostrils!

A guard ran through an archway. "They're all hatching, your lordship!" he shouted. He was trying to swat away a number of bat-sized baby dragons.

They swooped. They looped-the-loop. They dive-bombed the people in the court-yard below. They sneezed and breathed out fire.

"Aaaah," sighed Physic. "Aren't they sweet?"

"Arrgh!!" yelped Tom as one of them burnt his bottom.

Big Jim had tiny dragons flying around his head like a swarm of bees. He laughed heartily. "We did it, Robyn," he said. "We brought back dragons!"

Just then, one of the newly-hatched red dragons landed on Tom's shoulder and began nibbling his ear.

Lord Dashwood roared with laughter too. "I don't believe it!" he said. "Only the Green Men of Gressingham could succeed in catching the wild goose on a wild goose chase!"

An Afterword

And so it was that Tom became a squire and each of the Green Men became a knight: Sir Jim, Sir Physic, Sir Friendly, Sir Squat, Sir Lanky and so on. Lord Dashwood also awarded the men some land to go with their titles. He gave them Gressingham Forest.

Robyn-in-the-Hat did not accept any title or reward. How could she, without revealing her true identity? She already had a title of her own, for all they knew.

The Green Men were sent on many quests in their new role as knights, but Sir Fidget and Sir Friendly often stayed behind. They had important duties of their own along with Stubborn. The two knights and the mule were nursemaids to a clutch of growing youngsters: the famous Red Dragons of Gressingham.

Barrington Stoke would like to thank all its readers for commenting on the manuscript before publication and in particular:

Joseph Ball

Roisin Banks

Jenny Bullen

David Clark

Carole Clohery

Matthew Crowley

Nathan Duncan

Josie Guinness

Theo Guinness

E.R. Holland

John Hutchison

Declan McCabe

Neil Musk

Catherine Noel

Timmy Noel

Claire Nolan

Daniel Sanjay Patel

Lorraine Payne

Liberty Gettard Pickering

Jake Reynolds

Jake Swappsweet

Benny Owen Seeds

Megan Shemmell

Karen Tang

Charlotte Warr

Become a Consultant!

Would you like to give us feedback on our titles before they are published? Contact us at the email address below – we'd love to hear from you!

info@barringtonstoke.co.uk
www.barringtonstoke.co.uk